With love to Spiro and Blossom

First published in the United States 1991
by Dial Books
A Division of Penguin Books USA Inc.
375 Hudson Street · New York, New York 10014

Published in Great Britain 1990
by William Collins Sons & Co. Ltd.

First Edition
1 3 5 7 9 10 8 6 4 2

Library of Congress Cataloging in Publication Data
Ivory, Lesley Ann.
Cats in the sun / Lesley Anne Ivory.
p.   cm.
Summary: Text and illustrations depict cats enjoying the sunshine.
ISBN 0-8037-0955-2
1. Cats—Juvenile literature.
2. Cats—Pictorial works—Juvenile literature. [1. Cats.]
I. Title
SF445.7.I86 1991   636.8—dc20   90-43068   CIP   AC

CATS IN THE SUN

Lesley Anne Ivory

DIAL BOOKS NEW YORK

What a happy sight it is to see a cat enjoying the sunshine. Cats adore the sun and seek it everywhere. They appreciate the warmth left by the sun's rays on pebbled paths. They lie in pools of sunlight cast by the winter sun through windows onto rich carpets.

I seek cats wherever I go. Like cats, I also seek warm, sunny places—especially to enjoy holidays in—and I never have difficulty in finding furry friends. I find them on docks watching fishing boats in little Greek harbors . . .

or by the side of small, narrow streets, feeding their kittens in sunny corners.

I love the way the sun shines through their ears, making them seem almost lighted up from within. And I love the way the sun sometimes catches the outline of their fur and whiskers. If you look closely into cats' coats while they are basking in the sunshine, you can see many colors highlighted there, making each hair into a miniature rainbow.

They stretch and wash their faces on doorsteps, walls, and windowsills, enjoying the first rays of the sun, or waiting patiently and hopefully for something interesting to come along. Cats have lots of time.

Butterflies are born into sunlight and fascinate cats who watch them fluttering about, and who then leap like ballet dancers, trying to catch them as they fly. Usually butterflies are just too elusive to be caught, but I have known my little Motley (herself a small tortoiseshell) to successfully bring one down with her paws.

Cats use warm, sunny days as an excuse to sprawl in your best flowers in the garden—preferably catmint which they adore—rolling over and spoiling the shape of the plant by flattening it as they writhe about on their shoulder blades, wild with joy at the fragrant smell of the crushed leaves and flowers.

In North Africa I found two nests of kittens outside one cafe.
One was in a hedge of hibiscus in full bloom, and when
I looked more closely the mother cat looked out and I could
see four little faces peering at me through the exotic flowers.
The other nest was in a tiled recess which had had geraniums,
before the mother cat flattened them to furnish the "cot" for her
babies. I visited this cafe twice a day for a week, for coffee
and tea, but really to see how the kittens were getting on. The
owner of the cafe said, "You can have a kitten, no problem!"
"Oh yes, there is a problem," said my husband.
"She already has twelve at home!"

I have found cats sunbathing on famous, sun-warmed mosaics made by the Romans many years ago. I wonder how many cats have enjoyed the warmth of these little stones, and if they are even aware of the lovely intricate pictures and designs that made the floors of houses in days long past. Ancestral tigers and birds and fish and wonderfully patterned borders are now exposed to the sun, many pieces lost through the ages.

Thousands of miles away in my garden at home, Malteazer is also enjoying the warmth of the sunshine, and rolling over on a mosaic I once made, using little fragments of broken china I found in ploughed fields. My mosaic will not last as long as the Roman ones. It is already cracking, but Malteazer does not mind.

We once shared a lovely picnic on the shore of a Greek island with a family of cats who kept fetching more and more of their relatives when they found our picnic sufficiently tasty to be interesting.

Afterward everyone else fell asleep in the shade of a nearby olive tree.
I was looking at the interesting shells and stones and pieces of old pots
half sunken in the warm sand. Some hens and a magnificent cockerel
appeared and joined the cats to help clear up the crumbs, all among the
pink, wild beach flowers and grasses.

At the end of the day when the sun is setting, cats may be seen making
the most of the last little corners still in sunlight, washing their paws
and faces until the shadows lengthen, and the sun slopes around the other
side of the world to awaken all the cats there.